Stop, Train, Stop!

A Thomas the Tank Engine Story

Based on *The Railway Series*
by the Rev. W. Awdry

Illustrated by Owain Bell

BEGINNER BOOKS   A Division of Random House, Inc.

Thomas the Tank Engine & Friends

A BRITT ALLCROFT COMPANY PRODUCTION

Based on The Railway Series by the Rev W Awdry. Copyright © Gullane (Thomas) LLC 1995.
All rights reserved under International and Pan-American Copyright Conventions.
Published in the United States by Random House, Inc., New York, and simultaneously in
Canada by Random House of Canada Limited, Toronto.

www.randomhouse.com/kids
www.thomasthetankengine.com

RANDOM HOUSE and colophon are registered trademarks of Random House, Inc.

Library of Congress Cataloging-in-Publication Data
Stop, train, stop! : a Thomas the Tank Engine story / illustrated by Owain Bell. p. cm. "Based
on the Railway series by the Rev. W. Awdry." SUMMARY: When Thomas the Tank Engine decides
not to make his usual station stops one day, he learns that faster is not always better.
ISBN: 0-679-85806-7 (trade) — ISBN 0-679-95806-1 (lib. bdg.) [1. Railroads—Trains—Fiction.]
I. Bell, Owain, ill. II. Awdry, W. Railway series. PZ7.S88355 1995 [E]—dc20 94-15129

Printed in the United States of America   35

Stop, Train, Stop!

A Thomas the
Tank Engine Story

Every day Thomas the Tank Engine
chugged from the start of his line
to the end of his line
and back again.
"All aboard!"
called the little blue engine's conductor.

Every day Thomas and his coaches
puffed along,
not too fast...
not too slow...
and stopped at every station.

They stopped at Knapford,
where a little boy waved.

KNAPFORD

They stopped at Elsbridge,
where a spotted cow mooed.

They stopped at Hackenbeck.
People got on.
People got off.

One morning
the little blue engine said,
"I am tired
of making stops.
I am going to go
from the start of the line
to the end of the line
without stopping."

Clackety-clack!
Clackety-clack!
Away went the train
without looking back.

The little blue engine
whizzed right by Knapford.
The little boy
hardly had time to wave.

In the dining car,
passengers bounced
up and down in their seats.

"Stop, train, stop!
Stop on the spot!
Our hot food's cold
and our cold food's hot!"

But the train didn't stop.
It whizzed right by Elsbridge.
The spotted cow
hardly had time to moo.

In the sleeping car,
passengers bounced
up and down in their beds.

But the train didn't stop.
It whizzed right by Hackenbeck.
People could not get on.
People could not get off.

In the baggage car,
trunks and bags and pets
bounced all around.

Splish! A fish splashed
into a cat carrier.

Meow! A cat tumbled
into a bird cage.

Squawk! A bird flew
into a suitcase.
"Stop!" they called.
"Stop, train, stop!"

But the little blue engine
and the long brown coaches
didn't stop until—
SCREECH!—

they reached
the very last station.

The train had gone all the way
from the start of the line
to the end of the line
without stopping once.

The passengers
were not pleased!
Their soup was cold.
Their ice cream was hot.

Dresses were here.
Suits were there.
Fish wagged their tails.
Cats flew everywhere!

And Thomas the Tank Engine
did not feel happy either.
He said, "I miss boys waving.
I miss cows mooing.
I miss people getting on
and people getting off."

So from then on,
every day,
the train
traveled not too fast...
and not too slow...

KNAPFORD

and stopped at
every station.

"Go, train, go!"

I CAN READ IT ALL BY MYSELF

Beginner Books